# The Miracles of
# Sai Baba

# CONTENTS

1.      Sai begins his Journey     7

2.      Sai's Love and Compassion for Humanity     13

3.      "Selfless service purifies the mind."     20

4.      "Leaving out your pride and egoism,     22
   you should surrender yourself to me."

5.      "I never neglect you but protect you at all times."     25

6.      "Think of Him always. He will take care of you."     27

7.      "Do not fear. I myself am here, guarding you at all times."     30

8.      "He will come to your rescue in times of trouble."     33

9.      "In Truth all religions unite."     35

10.      "As you have sought My Protection, I would cross even beyond     37
    seven seas to help you."

11.      "If anyone is intolerant, unkind or     39
    insulting towards you, do not retaliate."

12.      "Whosoever brings his hands together in devotion,     41
    I shall reach him wherever he is.

13.      "All animals have a soul like us, we must treat     43
    them equally and feed them."

14.      "God runs to His devotees to help     46
    them in times of danger."

15.      "The Lord is the Protector of all."     48

| 16. | "Sacrifice, penance and knowledge are the means to attain God." | 50 |
| 17. | "One who lives in My remembrance... I am the bonded slave of his devotion." | 52 |
| 18. | "Believe in Me, remain fearless and have no anxiety." | 54 |
| 20. | "Worship of the Guru is equivalent to worshipping all the deities, for in the Guru, all the deities dwell." | 56 |
| 21. | "If wealthy, be humble." | 58 |
| 22. | "The Lord will protect him who possesses faith and patience." | 60 |
| 23. | "Have faith in me and none can deceive you." | 62 |
| 24. | "I never expect anything from you other than *Shraddha* and *Saburi*." | 64 |
| 25. | "Fortunate are those who hold my name close to their tongues." | 67 |
| 26. | "Do not wail, wait a bit and have patience. Your wish will be fulfilled." | 68 |
| 27. | "If you chant 'Sai Ram' daily, your mind will find peace and you will be greatly benefited." | 71 |
| 28. | "Give me one and receive tenfold." | 72 |
| 29. | "People must have full faith in the Lord's *Leela*." | 76 |
| 30. | "Abandon lust, wrath and avarice as they lead to self-destruction." | 78 |
| 31. | "I speak the Truth, nothing but the Truth." | 81 |
| 32 | "Believe Me, though I pass away." | 83 |

# Foreword

Popularly known as Shirdi Ke Sai Baba, Sai Baba was one of the most outstanding figures of his age. Believed to be an incarnation of Lord Shiva, Sai Baba walked this earth teaching brotherhood and unity amongst his fellowmen. Baba dedicated his life to bring about communal harmony between the Hindus and Muslims. Although he spent his life as a simple village *fakir* in Shirdi, his name and teachings spread far and wide to many parts of the world.

Baba's compassion and humanity were boundless. His devotees thrived on his teachings, his miracles and his goodness. His divinity was seen through the countless miracles that he performed. He would cure his devotees from all sorts of ailments that were incurable. Mentally and emotionally as well, he was a divine healer. Through his spiritual teachings, he helped his devotees attain contentment and peace within themselves.

To many, he was the 'Divine Gardener', the *Jagadguru* (Guru of the world) and the 'jewel'. His teachings were very simple; they included the basic principles of love, kindness, forgiveness and of course, devotion to God. "I reside where there is boundless faith," as he calls upon his devotees.

His teachings, till today, continue to guide millions of devotees around the world.

## Sai Begins his Journey

As much as we know about his teachings, Sai Baba's history before he reached Shirdi is vague. No one really knows much about the saint's childhood or where he came from. His story began when he reached Shirdi as a young lad of sixteen.

Sai Baba reached Shirdi dressed as a *fakir*, in a *kafni*. He had travelled for several days in search of his destination until he ultimately reached Shirdi where he settled himself under a *neem* tree seated in an *asana*.

People wondered where he was from and what he was doing there. They observed that there was something different about this boy of sixteen. He seemed more like a saint as he had both the look of an innocent child and that of an old man who was full of wisdom.

From then on, he stayed in Shirdi performing great miracles until the time he became known what he is known to us today – Sai Baba of Shirdi.

One day, as he sat under the *neem* tree and meditated, a troubled man, by the name of Chand Patil, came to him for help.

"Oh! Great one! Please help me," begged the man as he fell down to his knees.

"I have lost my horse and have been trying to find it for some days now. I fear that it has lost its way somewhere or perhaps has got caught in some terrible misfortune. Please help me find it."

Sai took one look at the man and saw the sincerity in his eyes. He did not utter a word. All of a sudden, he looked the other way as if he was waiting for someone to come. To the man's surprise, it was his horse that Baba was looking at!

"It is a miracle," thought Chand Patil as he watched his horse galloping towards him. He thanked the saint and asked for his blessings as he set out on his journey.

News of this incident did not take long to spread. Soon, other people started visiting him to seek his help and blessings.

Sai then set out to look for a place to stay in Shirdi. He saw that the people needed his help and went towards a village temple. There was a priest outside the temple. "Who are you and what do you want here, boy?" he asked.

"My master is Allah and I have come to seek shelter here in your temple," replied Sai.

"No! If your master is Allah then you cannot stay here. This is a temple for Hindus only and no Muslim shall be allowed to enter," said the priest.

Upon hearing this, Sai said, "Then I shall not worry you, priest. I can go and look for shelter in the Dwarkamai Masjid. I shall only leave you with this thought that God is the same everywhere. He lives in both temples and mosques." Sai walked away with a smile not showing any anger or resentment towards the priest.

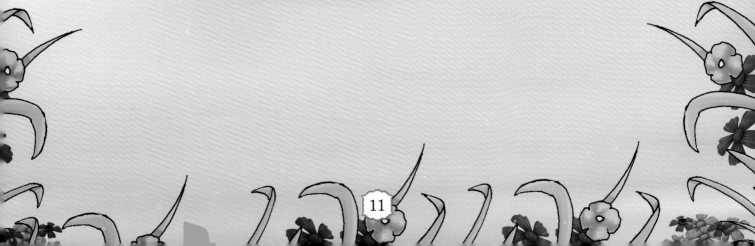

On reaching Dwarkamai, he went inside and found in it a home. From then on, Sai lived in the mosque. Sai became widely known to everyone in Shirdi. He was a miraculous healer, a wise saint and a selfless devotee of God.

Religion did not place any barriers. He treated Hindus as well as Muslims alike, with kindness. And it is with him, during this period, that the people too began to see no differences between the two.

# Sai's Love and Compassion for Humanity

Sai Baba was a gentle and compassionate man. He was always ready and willing to help those who were in need. The sick and ailing would always turn to him and he would do his best to help them get better.

He gently tended a leper's sores and nursed him till he got better while the rest of the people from the village hesitated to go near him.

Sai led a very simple life at the village. For whatever good he did, he never expected anything in return.

For food, he would go to a few houses in the neighbourhood and beg.

Some women would turn him away at times, but he would gently plead them, saying. "You have so much food in your kitchen, why can't you spare some for a *fakir*."

Sai was always so gentle in his speech that upon hearing his words, the women would fall to the ground and touch his feet. And of course, give him much more food than he could eat!

Not only did he collect food for himself, but also for the poor. Sai was a very caring man and whatever he got through begging from the houses in the neighbourhood, he shared with poor people he met along the way. Sometimes, he would remain hungry himself, so that he would be able to feed the needy.

Sai also spent some of his time, in the mornings, in the Lendi Gardens. There, he would be busy planting trees and flowers of different varieties. And whatever he planted and sowed always blossomed into beautiful plants, flowers or fruits.

It was here that he also came to be known as the 'Divine Gardener'.

Sai was very fond of the company of children and would sit outside most of the day, when he was not busy helping someone. He would tell them about God and of how both Ram and Rahim are the same but with different names. The children were drawn towards his pure heart and simplicity.

## "Selfless service purifies the mind."

One day, during the festival of *Diwali*, Sai Baba had given permission to the people to celebrate the festival at the mosque. So people started decorating the mosque and prepared the feast. However, they found that there was no mustard oil to light the lamps with. So Sai set out to the shopkeepers to ask for some oil. But the shopkeepers refused to help him.

Sai Baba simply laughed at their rudeness and walked away.

Now the shopkeepers, satisfied that they had deprived Sai of the mustard oil, wanted to go and see how he would light the lamps without the oil.

Upon reaching the Dwarkamai mosque, Sai directly started working and instead of putting oil into the lamps, he put water. The shopkeepers who had been watching from a close distance obviously were shocked to see this. They did not know what he was up to. He then put the cotton into the lamps and started lighting them one by one. The shopkeepers began to think that he had gone mad and started laughing.

To their great surprise, the lamps started to glow. It was a miracle! As they stood staring, the entire mosque lit up and shone brightly. They then realised what they had done and immediately felt sorry.

They went to Sai Baba and fell on their knees.

"Forgive us, O great one! We are but sinners!" they said.

Sai Baba smiled and said, "I appreciate you for having accepted your mistakes, for that is the only way to correct them."

# "Leaving out your pride and egoism, you should surrender yourself to me."

A certain young *tehsildar* invited his friend, who was a doctor, to accompany him to Shirdi. While the *tehsildar* was a devotee of Sai Baba, the doctor was a great devotee of Lord Rama.

On reaching Shirdi, the *tehsildar* said, "Since we are here in Shirdi, let us go to Sai Baba and seek his blessings."

"No! I am a devotee of Lord Rama and I shall bow down to him alone. Besides, I do not think it would be suitable for me to bow down before a *fakir*," replied the doctor.

"If you don't want to bow down before Sai, you do not have to. Even Sai would not want that," assured his friend.

As soon as they entered the mosque, the doctor ran and threw himself at the feet of Sai Baba. Sai Baba smiled at him knowingly and blessed him.

The *tehsildar* was shocked and on their way back home he asked the doctor, "What made you bow before Baba? I thought that you did not think it's appropriate to bow before a *fakir*?"

With tears of joy, the doctor answered, "I really don't understand what happened. All I know is that when we entered, I did not see Sai Baba but Lord Ram of Ayodhya. It was a miracle."

Thus saying, he thanked his friend, for he had never had such a feeling of bliss and contentment before.

From then on, he became one of Sai's fervent devotees.

23

# "I never neglect you but protect you at all times."

One summer in the village of Shirdi, at harvest time, Baba called on a farmer who had been busy in the fields the whole year. He woke up with a feeling that something bad would happen to this man and his crops, and called him to warn him.

"Go to your fields fast! There is a fire that has just started and it may ruin your crops," said Sai Baba.

The farmer believed the saint and ran to his field. However, on reaching there, he found no fire. He looked everywhere, but there was no fire. His farm was just as he had left it. Puzzled by what Sai had told him, he returned to Sai to inform him that there was no fire and there was no need to worry.

Just as he had told the saint that there was no fire, Baba said, "Go run quickly to your farm. It is under fire now! Go and save your crops."

Again, the farmer ran back to his fields. The moment he reached, he saw that Sai was right. There was a fire raging in his field and it was destroying his crops.

He cried "Help! Help!"

People from the neighbouring fields ran to help but they could not put out the fire.

Suddenly the farmer remembered Baba and knew that it was only him who would be able to save his harvest. So he rushed back to Sai Baba and urged him to come.

Sai Baba agreed and when he reached the field, all he did was sprinkle some water on the fire.

"Stop! Stop destroying this poor farmer's harvest," commanded Sai. The fire ceased to burn his crops and went off almost immediately. It was a miracle!

Overwhelmed by gratitude, the farmer fell on his knees and said, "Long live Sai Baba!"

# "Think of Him always. He will take care of you."

Once, a young girl was seriously ill with tuberculosis and there was no hope for her to live. As her last wish, she had requested her family members to take her to the Dwarkamai mosque so that she could for once see the virtuous Sai Baba of Shirdi whom she had heard so much about. So the girl's relatives agreed to take her to visit Sai.

When Sai Baba saw the girl and how weak she was, he was full of sympathy towards her.

"Why did you bring the girl all the way to Shirdi in this condition? Take her back home immediately and let her rest. Be sure to keep her warm when you reach home and feed her only water."

The family obeyed Baba's instructions and took her home, feeding her only water and after seven days, she died.

On the day of her death, Sai Baba was still sleeping. It was morning and Sai did not wake up at the usual time. He had overslept and this surprised everyone as he usually woke up at the same time every morning.

Meanwhile, the girls' family was preparing for her funeral.

Everyone was in grief. Yet, as they laid her body on the funeral pyre, it seemed as if the girl was moving. All of a sudden, the girl got up and woke from the dead. Everyone was shocked and wondered how this was possible.

The girl then spoke and said, "There was a horrible man who was trying to drag me somewhere. I called Baba for help and he came and beat up the man. Then he took me to the *Chawari*."

The girl described the *Chawari*. Her vivid description of the *Chawari* was amazing since she had not ever seen it before.

This was another one of Baba's miracles!

The girl's disease had disappeared and everyone was happy. Another life had been saved by Baba.

# "Do not fear. I myself am here, guarding you at all times."

Sai Baba was known for his miracles in helping people from Shirdi and all over. When there was an epidemic of cholera in the areas around Shirdi, a large number of people were infected and died.

The people in Shirdi became scared lest the disease spread to their village as well. There was panic everywhere and everyone felt helpless.

So the people turned to Sai Baba and asked him for his help.

"There will no longer be any deaths from this disease," assured Sai.

Sai had told the people that he would stop this disease from spreading as well as provide a cure for those already suffering from this disease.

So he went straight to work. He asked his pupil to bring him a grinding mill and wheat. When he got the items, he started grinding the wheat into flour. Everyone asked him what he was doing.

"I am preparing the medicine that will get rid of the epidemic once and for all," was the reply.

He then told his pupil to take the flour and sprinkle it everywhere around the village.

News that Baba had prepared the medicine spread fast in the village and soon everyone knew about it. People in Shirdi as well as those outside the village rushed to him to take some of the medicine.

So strong was their faith in the saint that all helped to scatter the medicine everywhere around the village.

In no time, people were cured and the disease was gone.

Baba's fame spread far and wide and Shirdi also grew. Many became his *bhaktas* and soon Shirdi came into prominence.

# "He will come to your rescue in times of trouble."

Baba never delivered long sermons. His lessons were simple parables which won the hearts of all listeners.

One day, when he and his followers were assembled together, a noisy commotion interrupted their session. There was a confusion about someone having been bitten by a snake.

Sai immediately ran out and asked, "What happened?"

"Shama has been bitten by a snake. It's not an ordinary snake, but the most poisonous snake, the snake *Gokharu*," came a voice from the crowd.

Shama was brought before Sai Baba by his relatives and they begged him to save the boy.

"Do not worry, nothing will happen to your son," Sai consoled the mother who was weeping amongst the crowd.

He then massaged Shama's foot as he began to speak, "Come out of this body and leave Shama. Come out!"

Sai chanted these words over and over again as if urging the poison to leave the man's body.

Slowly and miraculously, the poison started dropping out of the wound and in no time, Shama got up and walked by himself as if he had never been bitten by any snake! It was a miracle! The people shouted in praise of Sai when they saw this for they knew how great he was, "Hail Sai Baba! Hail."

# "In Truth all religions unite."

Sai Baba welcomed both Hindus and Muslims to the mosque. He had *bhaktas* from both religions.

One day, while he was having a conversation with one of the pupils, a small child came to the mosque and gave the saint some flowers. Baba thanked the boy and blessed him before he left. From that day onwards, many Hindu devotees came to worship him at the mosque.

They were welcomed just as the Muslims were. People were living together despite their differences. There was no other time when both Hindus and Muslims lived so well alongside each other.

However, a certain Muslim devotee who, although, respected Sai deeply, felt it was not right for Hindus to come and do their *pooja* at the mosque.

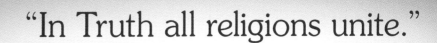

35

This disturbed Sai who believed that Ram and Rahim were one and the same.

He said, "My child, is it so bad that people come to worship me at the mosque? The only reason why they come here is because this is where I live. So, I am the cause of that, and if you have any problem with the Hindus coming to mosque then you should kill me."

Sai's calm response to his problem incited the devotee's anger even more.

He took out his stick and tried to hit Sai on the head with it. But Sai was quick and gripped the man's wrist. The moment Sai held him, the man fell to the ground.

Sai's grip was so strong that it could have been nothing but some supernatural power.

Since then, the man never dared to utter a word against Sai. He had learnt his lesson and soon got rid of his feelings of hatred and revenge and began to live alongside both Muslim and Hindu devotees of Sai.

## "As you have sought My Protection...
## I would cross even beyond seven seas to help you."

Baba had a number of disciples following him.

One day, one of his most favourite disciples, Tatya, had fallen sick. He had not come to the mosque for several days and Baba became worried.

So Baba decided to pay a visit to Tatya at his home. Sai set out, concerned for his dear disciple and his mother, taking with him some *udi* from the *dhuni* lit at the Dwarkamai and went on his way.

When Baba reached Tatya's house, he saw him lying on the bed looking weak and in pain. His mother was sitting beside him and she too looked distressed.

"Please save my son," begged the mother, "He has high fever and has been asleep all these days."

Sai went closer to his disciple and he gently massaged the *udi* on his forehead.

Moments after Sai had massaged the *udi* onto Tatya's forehead, he regained consciousness. He uttered, "Sai Baba" and then he opened his eyes.

Baba was glad to see his dear devotee awake and said to him, "I have been waiting for you, but since you could not come to me, I came to you."

Tatya of course could not understand or explain what happened. "All I remember is lying down to sleep after I had returned from meeting you and now I am awake," said Tatya, confused.

"You have had very high fever all these days. Then Baba came this morning and cured you from the sickness," explained the mother.

"Thank you, Baba. Thank you for saving my life!" said Tatya.

After Baba saved the life of his favourite disciple, Tatya, news of the miraculous *udi* spread fast. More people began to visit Shirdi, not only to seek Sai Baba's blessings but the sick and the ailing also visited Shirdi especially so that they could get treated by the extraordinary *udi*.

# "If anyone is intolerant, unkind or insulting towards you, do not retaliate."

Amongst the many that went for the *udi* was an unfortunate man who had a blind mother and a lame sister. His wife was found to have tuberculosis so he took her to be treated by the priest of the village who was also a physician.

The physician however was extremely jealous of Sai Baba. He was furious when he found out that this man was also a devotee of Sai Baba.

"Since you are such a great follower of Sai Baba, what are you doing here with me? I refuse to treat your wife any longer. Go and take her, along with your mother and sister, to your great Sai Baba and never show your face here again!" said the physician to the man.

Upon reaching the Dwarkamai mosque, the man fell down on his knees before Sai Baba and touched his feet. He told him about his family and begged the saint to cure them.

The man had great faith in Sai Baba. He was not worried that the priest had refused to treat his wife and that he threw him out of the temple. All that mattered to him was that he had made it to the home of Sai Baba, certain that Sai would be able to help him.

Taking out three packets of *udi*, Sai said, "Take these three packets of *udi*. One should be given to your wife. Use the second packet and rub on your sister's feet and give the third packet to your mother. She can use it for washing her eyes. Just remember that it was your faith that led you here, it is also your faith that will help you."

The man thanked Sai and went home.

He did as he was told with the *udi*. His mother's vision was restored, his sister walked and his wife was no longer sick.

Sai's miracle unfolded before his eyes.

# "Whosoever brings his hands together in devotion, I shall reach him wherever he is."

Even though Sai spent most of his time indoors, at the Dwarkamai mosque, he was very much in touch with what was going on outside. He knew whenever his devotees were in trouble and needed his help and he would always make sure that he would be able to help them.

One day as he was sitting by the fire with a few of his *bhaktas*, all of a sudden he stared into the fire and looked blank. His devotees were wondering what had happened to him and they asked, "What is the matter, Baba?"

Baba did not answer. Instead he extended his hand into the fire as if he was taking something out. Everyone was shocked to see this behaviour and quickly pulled out his hand out of the fire lest he burnt himself. But no one dared to ask him why he did so.

Two days after this incident, there came a letter to the mosque, addressed to Sai Baba. Sai asked one of his devotees to read the letter out loud for him. The letter read:

"My dearest Baba,

I bow before you, O Great one! I am your firm *bhakta*.

My faith in you increases everyday. I am writing this letter to you to praise and honour you for the miracle you had performed in my house.

Being a blacksmith, one day, I was straightening a red hot rod of iron. My wife was by the furnace and she held our child in her arms. All of a sudden, the child leaped into the fire! I quickly pulled him out of the fire but during the process I was praying to you.

You did hear me and answered my prayers. Because of you, my child is safe with no bruises, injuries or even a small blister. It was a miracle.

Hail Sai Baba. May you live forevermore!"

When the disciples heard this, their faith increased even more. And so did it happen with the millions of other devotees who heard the story.

# "All animals have a soul like us, we must treat them equally and feed them."

Sai Baba encouraged humanity and compassion among his devotees. The same way he treated them with kindness, he expected them to treat each other.

The devotees were so encouraged by Sai's teachings that most of them were helpful and caring towards others. One day, as a woman was preparing food, a stray dog came to her door. When she saw the dog, she immediately felt pity for it as it looked like it had not eaten for days. She looked at her own plate and although she was feeling hungry, decided to give the food to the dog. "I can eat later again; let me feed this poor dog now. He seems to be starving," thought the woman.

The dog ate hungrily and went away.

Later in the evening, she went to the Dwarkamai mosque to see Sai Baba.

When Sai saw her, he smiled and looked at her with great affection. He then said, "Thank you for your kindness this morning."

Puzzled, the woman said, "I am sorry, but perhaps you are mistaken, I did not meet you this morning," said the woman.

"This morning, you gave food to a stray dog. It was I who came to you in the form of a dog, my child. You treated me with kindness. All living creatures are God's creations. By serving God's creations, you serve Him," said Sai Baba to the woman. When the woman heard this, she fell to his knees. "Long live Sai Baba," she cried.

# "God runs to His devotees to help them in times of danger."

Once there was a poor man who was heavily in debt. The moneylender had given him only a few days till he could pay his dues. The farmer tried many ways to come up with money to clear his debt, but the debt was a great sum for him to clear in a short period of time.

He was extremely worried and sad and was constantly haunted by visions of the moneylender coming to him asking for money.

A day before the money was due, the moneylender did visit the man. "I have just come to inform you that I shall come to collect the money that you owe me tomorrow morning. I hope you'll have it ready by then. Otherwise, I'll have you arrested!" threatened the moneylender.

The man was terrified. He could not eat nor sleep.

All of a sudden, he remembered Sai Baba and prayed for his help.

The next morning, he was visited by the son of an old friend. "I have come to ask for your help. I have some money here and I want to invest it in some business," said the young man. "Will you please help me? Since my father is no more, you are the only person I can trust."

"My son, I am the last person you should be asking. I myself am heavily in debt and I cannot repay the money. By this afternoon, I shall be in prison," said the man.

"Then you should use this money to pay your debts. You are a friend of my father's. How can I not help you?" offered the young man.

The man refused at first but on his persistent insistence, he accepted the money and was able to pay off the debt.

As he left, the young man said, "Baba has sent me here for a reason, and I am glad to have fulfilled it."

After this miracle, the man knew the greatness of Sai, for he had seen it with his own eyes!

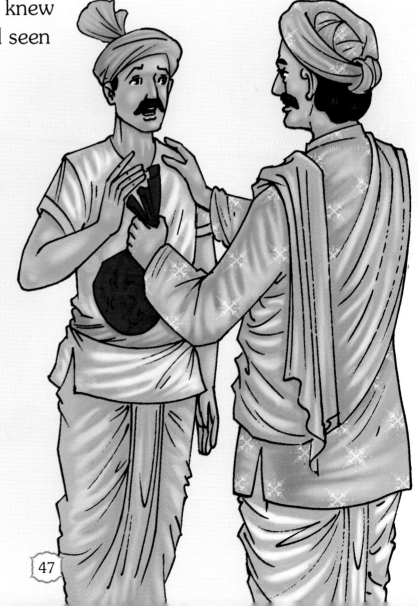

# "The Lord is the Protector of all."

Sai Baba's greatness spread to different parts of the country rapidly, especially with the popularity of the splendid and inimitable *kirtans* spread by his devotees. Baba's fame reached a helpless man who had a sick child. He had sought medicine from everywhere but could not find the right cure. Now, he could only rely on religion. When he heard about Sai Baba, he turned to his ailing child who frequently broke into fits and his mother who was struggling to control the disease; he decided that he must visit Shirdi with his family and try to get a cure for his son.

A few days later, along with his wife and ailing son, he headed to Shirdi. When they reached, they directly went to the Dwarkamai mosque. There, as soon as the man brought the child before Baba, the child immediately fainted. His mouth started foaming and his whole body started shaking and he was covered in sweat.

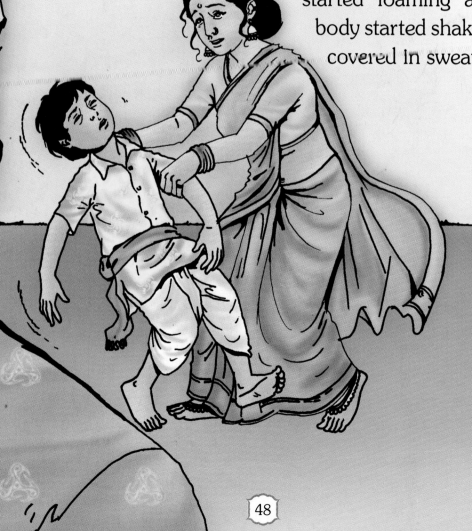

Although this happened to the boy frequently, the attack which he had this time was none like he ever had. This terrified his parents and the mother started wailing.

Seeing this, Sai Baba comforted the mother and said to her, "There is no need to fear. This attack is worse than before, I know, but you must have faith in me and I assure you that this is the last time he would be like this."

Just as he said that, the boy started to calm down. Both the parents were relieved and thankful towards Baba for his miracle. The boy's sickness disappeared. These are such instances that show Baba's greatness.

# "Sacrifice, penance and knowledge are the means to attain God."

Hundreds of miles away from Shirdi, in a village, lived a man named Cholkar who longed to see and pay respect to the great Sai Baba. Despite his desire to visit Shirdi however, he could not as he did not have money to travel so far.

Cholkar attended one of the discourses organised by Sai's devotees and he was deeply touched by Sai's words and teachings.

When he got home he could not stop talking about it to his wife. He expressed his longing to his wife.

"Let us pray that Baba hears you and helps you to clear this year's examination papers tomorrow," said the wife. "When you do pass that test, then we can go to Shirdi."

"We shall cut down on our spending and have tea without sugar from now onwards," decided Cholkar. Indeed, Baba did hear his prayers and Cholkar did pass the test!

After Cholkar had passed the test, he was entitled to a higher income and so he was able to save money. A day came when he had saved enough money for the trip and the couple

was very happy for they will be going to Shirdi, finally.

When they met Baba, the couple was overjoyed and fell to his feet.

Baba smiled and greeted them by their names. They were surprised at how he had recognised them as they had never met.

"You knew who I was when you saw me," explained Baba. "In the same way, I also know you."

Then he offered them tea with a little more sugar and smiled at them.

At this, Cholkar knew Baba's powers and understood that from then onwards he and his wife would never have to drink tea without sugar again because they had Sai Baba watching over them!

"One who lives in My remembrance... I am the bonded slave of his devotion."

A large number of people visited Shirdi. Most of them were Sai's devotees and he welcomed all.

Once a lawyer decided to go and visit Sai Baba.

A friend of his, who was also a devotee of Sai Baba, regretted the fact that he too was not able to join him. However, as a token of his devotion and respect towards the saint, he sent with his friend a coconut for Baba.

While on the long journey to Shirdi, without thinking twice, the lawyer took the coconut out of his bag, broke it and ate it up. He had completely forgotten his friend's sentiments regarding the coconut that he had sent for Sai Baba. It was only after he had eaten the coconut that he realised that it was meant for Baba.

On reaching Shirdi, the lawyer went straight to Sai Baba to pay his respects.

As he kneeled down on his knees, Baba looked at him and asked, "Where is the coconut that your friend, my brother sent for me?" The lawyer had no answer and stared blankly at Sai Baba.

He hung his head in shame and burst out into tears. "I have eaten it, Baba. I am a sinner. Please forgive me," cried the lawyer.

"I know," Baba looked at him and smiled. "Forget about this now. I am not angry. In fact, I am happy that it satisfied your hunger."

Merciful Baba forgave the lawyer and blessed him. The lawyer of course, learned his lesson and his resolute faith in Baba grew tenfold.

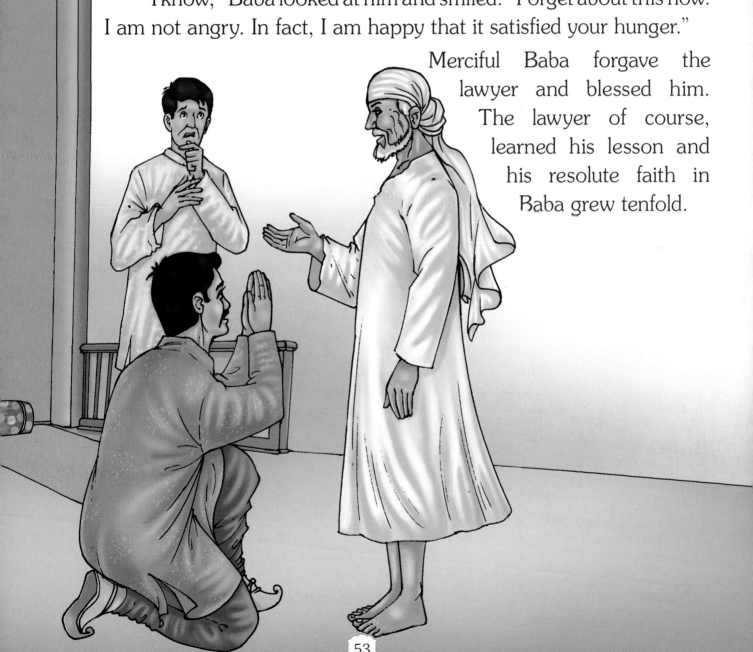

# "Believe in Me, remain fearless and have no anxiety."

Bayaja Bai was a dedicated devotee of Sai Baba. She was also the mother of his favourite disciple, Tatya. Bayaja Bai was actually more than a devotee to Sai Baba. She was more like a mother to him.

One day, he heard of news that she was unwell, so he rushed to meet her. He was disturbed to see that she looked frail and weak. He understood that her end was near.

"We are not immortal," thought Sai. The same day, she died and Sai Baba was heartbroken with this loss and so was her son, Tatya.

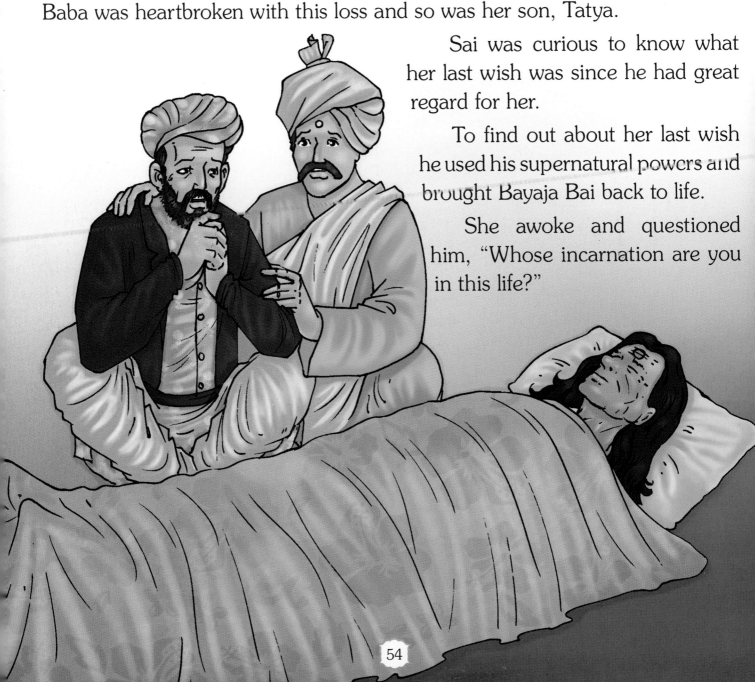

Sai was curious to know what her last wish was since he had great regard for her.

To find out about her last wish he used his supernatural powers and brought Bayaja Bai back to life.

She awoke and questioned him, "Whose incarnation are you in this life?"

"Mother, I am not an incarnation, I am only a son of God. I was sent to earth to wipe out sin, dishonesty, superstitions and other evil aspects of life. I was sent to lead the people to the path of love, kindness and humanity," replied Baba.

Bayaja Bai, then stated her last wish. "I only have one thing to ask of you Baba," she said.

"Speak. What is it that I can do for you?" enquired Baba.

"Tatya is a young man and without me, he will be completely alone. Please take care of him," pleaded the mother.

"Mother, he is my brother and I shall protect him. You have my word for it."

Bayaja Bai drew her last breath and passed away. And as for Sai Baba – he made sure that he kept his promise!

# "Worship of the Guru is equivalent to worshipping all the deities, for in the Guru, all the deities dwell."

Megha was an illiterate brahmin who knew nothing of his duties. He never performed any *pooja* nor did he know anything about the Vedas. His master, Hari Vinayak Sathe, a devotee of Sai Baba wanted him to recite certain *mantras*.

"Why don't you go and see Sai Baba since he is the living form of Lord Shiva?" he one day suggested to Megha. Megha had already heard so much about Sai Baba that he agreed.

However, as soon as he reached the mosque, Sai started chasing him away with a stick. "How dare you come in here, Megha?" shouted Sai Baba. "You are of high caste and I am of low caste. You should not have come here!"

Poor Megha ran out of the mosque, not understanding how Sai knew his name or why he chased him out.

After sometime, Baba calmed down and then called Megha back inside. Megha stayed in Shirdi for quite some time.

Megha was so touched by Baba's teachings that he became a devotee of the saint. On the day of one *Makar Sankranti*, Megha bathed Baba with the Godavari water. Instead of simply washing his head, Megha wanted to give him a complete bath. While doing so, he spoke, "I am pleased to bathe you with this holy water. Lord Shiva would be pleased too."

"Well, you can wash my head and that would be a complete bath," suggested Baba. He then sat down and allowed Megha to pour water.

When he was done however, he saw that it was just Baba's head that was wet while the rest of his body was completely dry.

"How could this be possible?" wondered the brahmin.

Yet, later he understood that he should not have tried to force Baba into receiving the bath. He went to ask for Sai's forgiveness and never disobeyed him again.

## "If wealthy, be humble."

Sai Baba had an innumerable number of devotees from many parts of the country. One amongst them was the wealthy Nana Sahib Chandorkar.

Nana and his wife were very generous and never refused any beggar anything.

Sai had noticed this generosity of theirs and felt that it could be taken advantage of. So, he told him, "Nana, your big-heartedness is greatly admirable but you must not give the beggars more than what they need. If they ask for more than what you have given, refuse them politely. Always remember, you should treat the poor with kindness."

One day, a beggar did come asking for alms. Nana's wife gave her alms. "More," said the beggar maid. Nana's wife again gave her some more alms.

Again she said, "More." This irritated Nana's wife and she said, "I think you have enough there. Now go away".

"No! I need more," said the woman, refusing to leave.

Nana's wife did not know what to do, so she called her husband.

Nana came and told her, "Get out of here woman! You have received enough alms already." Seeing that she refused, he sent his servants to throw her out.

A few days later, Nana went to visit Sai. Upon meeting him, he bowed before him but Sai simply ignored him.

"Are you angry with me, Baba?" asked Nana in confusion.

"You have broken your promise to treat beggars with kindness. There was no need to send your servants to throw that beggar maid out," said Sai.

Upon hearing this Nana fell to his knees and begged for forgiveness. Of course, the ever forgiving Baba took him in his arms and forgave him!

# "The Lord will protect him who possesses faith and patience."

Once there was a devotee of Sai Baba by the name of Chandrabai Borkar. Her husband, Ramchandra Borkar had fallen sick, so she prayed to Sai Baba to cure him. One night, Sai came to her in a dream, saying, "Mother, do not worry. Your husband will be alright. Just rub some *udi* on his forehead and he will be fine. But when he does get better, tell him not to leave the house before eleven 'o' clock in the morning."

Chandrabai woke up and immediately did as Sai had directed. In the morning, his illness was gone. But when Chandrabai warned him about going out before eleven 'o'clock, he paid no heed.

"It is all superstition," he said and he insisted on going to the office. So his wife accompanied him. The couple lived very close to the railway tracks which they had to cross to go to the town.

As they were crossing, Chandrabai's husband did not see the train coming from another side and was hit. Chandrabai fainted there on the spot. When she regained consciousness, she was told that her husband was fine except for his leg.

At home, Chandrabai said, "This only happened because you had disobeyed Baba's wish. Had you listened, this mishap would not have occurred. Still he saved you."

He still went to the doctor for treatment. The doctor's medicines failed.

"Let me apply some *udi* on your leg. Baba will cure you again," said Chandrabai.

Chandrabai's husband was silent. He thought, "It would be a miracle if this *udi* cured my leg."

Indeed it did! The next morning, the man felt better and soon enough he was completely cured! It was a miracle. From that day onwards, Chandrabai's husband never doubted the word of Sai Baba. The couple became true devotees of Sai Baba and visited Shirdi frequently.

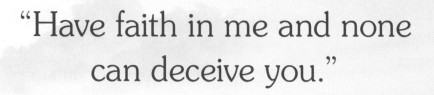

# "Have faith in me and none can deceive you."

Besides followers, there were also people who were curious about his supernatural powers and doubted the great Sai Baba.

One of them was Hari Kanoba who visited Shirdi mainly for the reason of finding out the secret of this saint's powers.

On one of these visits he wore a pair of new shoes. Before entering the mosque, he hid it in a corner so that no one would steal them. After his *darshan*, he went back to that same corner to take his shoes but was astonished to find the shoes missing from there. He searched everywhere, but he could not find them.

Moments after this, he saw a boy chanting, "Son of Hari with a turban of *zari*."

The boy was carrying a stick on his shoulder and at the end of the stick hung Hari Kanoba's shoes. Upon seeing this, he became furious and went towards the boy.

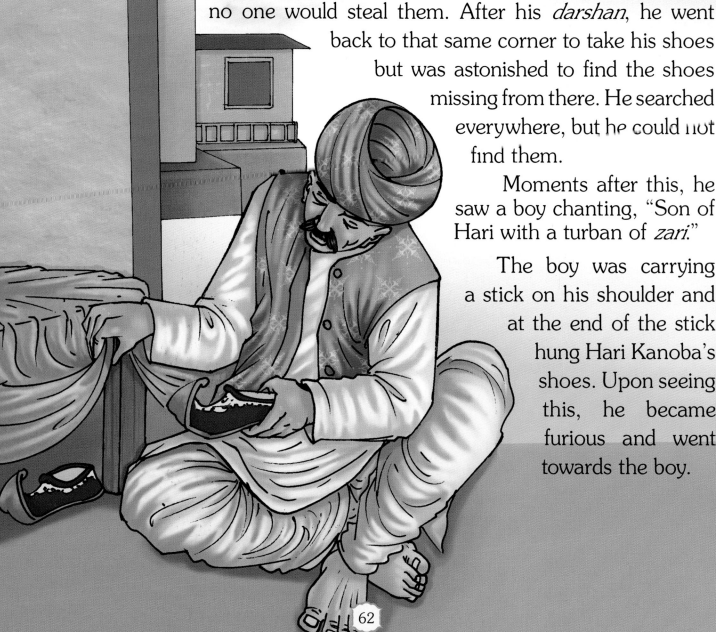

"Those are my shoes," he yelled. "Boy, come back here and give me back my shoes."

Though the boy stopped, he refused to return the shoes to the man.

"Sai Baba had told me to give these shoes to someone who is the son of a man who bears the initial 'K' in his name and who wears the turban of *zari*," replied the boy.

With this, Hari Kanoba took off his turban and humbly said, "My father's name is Kanoba and I am wearing the turban of *zari*."

He realised that this was Sai Baba's way of telling him not to doubt his powers and to have faith in him. The boy returned his shoes and as much as Hari tried to examine how Sai found out what was his father's name, he could not.

Indeed, the powers of Sai Baba were divine! Hari Kanoba became a devout follower of Sai Baba, thenceforth.

# "I never expect anything from you other than *Shraddha* and *Saburi*."

Once there were two friends named Sapatnekar and Shavde. They were both law students. One day, after they had both taken their bar examinations, they discussed the question paper and found out that Shavde had not done so well.

"What are you going to do if you don't pass this exam?" asked Sapatnekar.

"I will not pass this exam. Sai Baba has told me so. But he has said that I will pass next year and I have firm faith in him," replied Shavde.

Upon hearing this, Sapatnekar made fun of him and laughed at his friend for being superstitious. However, things did happen as Baba had foretold.

After the exam, they both went their separate ways.

Years later, Sapatnekar's only son died and left him heart broken. Seeking peace and solace, he visited many temples but all was in vain.

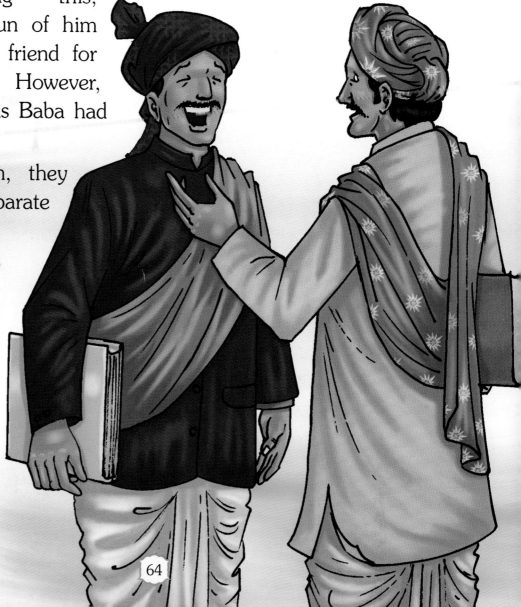

One day, he remembered his friend, Shavde, and how he talked about Sai Baba with such great reverence.

He thought, "Maybe I should visit Sai Baba of Shirdi and see if I can have peace after that."

So, he and his wife headed to Shirdi.

Sai saw them approaching from a distance but he did not let them enter. Again, they went the next day but still he did not meet them. They tried for several days but Sai Baba refused to meet them. They were very sad and decided to go back home.

One day, as Sapatnekar's wife was sleeping, she had a dream. In her dream, she saw a man with a cloth around his head. She was carrying a pitcher and the man said to her, "My child, why are you working so hard? Let me fill it for you." When she woke up, she told her husband. Sapatnekar believed that it was none other than Sai Baba. "We shall go and visit Sai Baba again tomorrow," said the husband, believing that this was a sign from the saint himself.

When they went to the mosque again, they finally met Sai Baba. Sapatnekar's wife went and bowed before Baba and he blessed her. Yet, when Sapatnekar went before him, he turned away. Sapatnekar wondered what he did wrong and suddenly remembered the day when he had ridiculed both Shavde and Sai Baba. He fell at Sai Baba's feet and begged for forgiveness. "I am a sinner, please forgive me," he said as tears rolled down his face.

Baba, seeing this, felt sorry for him. He blessed him and told him not to worry. "It was unfortunate that you lost your only son, I deeply feel for you. So, I am going to bless you with another child whom you will love and take care of," said Sai to the man.

A year later, Sapatnekar's wife did give birth to a child just as Sai had promised. The family became firm devotees of Sai Baba from then onwards and made frequent visits to Shirdi.

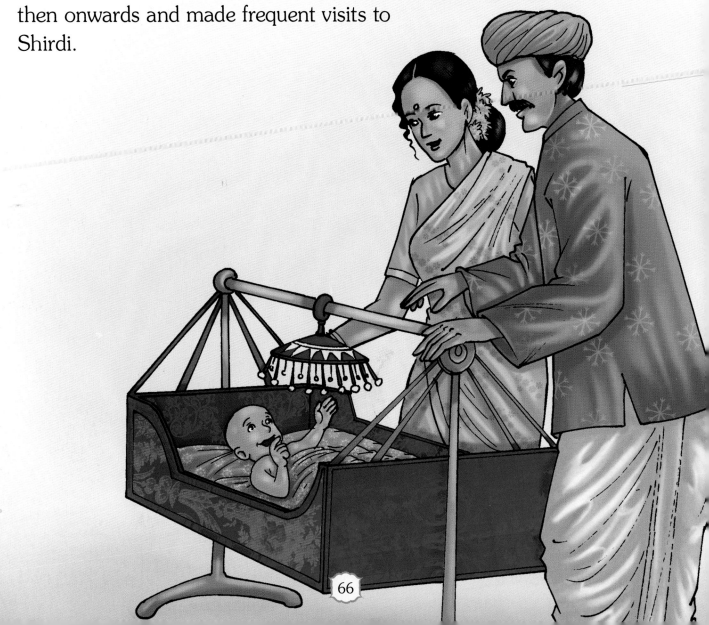

# "Fortunate are those who hold my name close to their tongues."

Although Sai Baba was always at one place most of the time, he always knew when his devotees needed his help.

Once there were two friends who went to Shirdi to visit Sai Baba. They stayed there for four days and each bought a picture of Sai Baba to take home.

On the way back, one of them was thinking of the picture of Sai and regretted not having bought another picture of Sai Baba for his brother as well.

When he reached home, he took out his picture so he could hang it at home.

To his surprise, he found two pictures. He ran out and went after his friend to ask him if he had forgotten to take his picture. The friend checked his bag and found his picture still there.

At this point, he realised that this could only be Sai Baba taking care of each of his devotees and fulfilling each of their needs.

# "Do not wail, wait a bit and have patience. Your wish will be fulfilled."

Besides being a great healer, Baba was also a wonderful teacher. He taught his devotees the importance of hard work. He could not tolerate laziness and idleness in his devotees. One day, he noticed that one of his devotees had become very sluggish. He did not want to work hard, despite the fact that he had a lot of land. Baba saw this land had gone to waste as there was no product that came out of it. One day, Baba called for him and told him, "There is a pot of gold in your fields. If you plough it, you will find it."

When the man heard this, he became excited and rushed to his land and started ploughing it. But he did not find any pot. Disappointed, he went back to the Dwarkamai and told Sai Baba that he could not find any pot there.

"Which direction did you plough?" asked Sai.

"I ploughed straight," replied the man.

"Oh, then you should have ploughed it horizontally. Go back to your fields and plough it horizontally this time. You are sure to get it," said Baba.

The man paid heed and went back to his fields. There, again he ploughed the field. He ploughed... and ploughed... and ploughed but found nothing. Again, he returned to the mosque and told Baba that he found nothing.

At this Baba said, "There is only one more thing you need to do," said Baba. "Go back to your field and sow chilly seeds. Then water it whenever necessary. There you will find your pot of gold."

When the man heard this, he finally understood what Baba was trying to tell him. He had so much land which was not put to any productive use. From then onwards, the man ploughed his fields regularly and indeed he acquired many pots of gold from it.

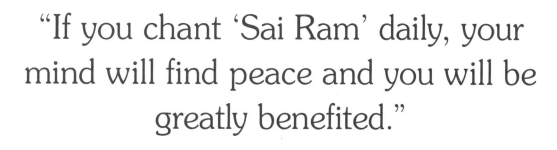

# "If you chant 'Sai Ram' daily, your mind will find peace and you will be greatly benefited."

A young doctor was travelling to Kopargaon on a bullock cart. With him, he had a few personal belongings and a bag which contained important documents. The road was very rough towards the destination, and the bag containing the documents fell off the cart.

When the doctor reached, he noticed his bag missing. He looked for it everywhere but the bag could not be found.

The doctor was miserable as the papers he had kept there were very important. In that dark hour, he had no one else to turn to except Baba. So that night he prayed to Sai Baba to help him find the bag.

The next morning he went to see a friend who was ill. He narrated to his friend how worried he was about his lost bag.

At that moment, the friend's maid overheard and interrupted the conversation and said, "My father found a bag yesterday on the road and it could be yours."

Then she ran out to bring the bag from her house. The doctor hoped and prayed that it was his bag that the girl's father had found.

The doctor's prayers were answered. He was fortunate as the bag was his. He looked inside and found all his papers just as he had kept them. He thanked the maid.

He was overjoyed and knew very well that it was the divine powers of Sai Baba that this was not just a coincidence but prayer from the heart. He could not stop thinking of the greatness of Sai Baba after that.

# "Give me one and receive tenfold."

One day, a devotee of Baba went to the Dwarkamai mosque to have a *darshan* of Sai Baba. Upon seeing him, Baba gave him his blessings and said to him, "Tomorrow, I shall come to your house and have dinner. Please prepare me a meal. I shall come along with two to three *fakirs*, so you can make enough food for us and your family."

When Sai said that, the devotee was so excited that he ran home to tell his wife.

The next day, towards dinnertime, the devotee was waiting anxiously for Baba by the door. Soon, five *fakirs* came, but Baba was not there. The *fakirs* were invited in and they sat down for a sumptuous meal.

The devotee continued to wait for Baba.

After some time, twenty more 'fakirs' came. When the couple saw the large number of people, they were worried that the food would not be enough. So, his wife went to the kitchen to see how much food was left. However, when she reached, she was shocked to see that the pots were still full. When her husband saw this he was even happier. He understood that this was only due to Sai's divine powers.

He ran to Dwarkamai mosque to invite Sai to have his meal but Sai replied saying, "I have been eating at your place the whole day and cannot eat anymore." When he said this, the devotee shouted, "All Hail, Sai Baba!" He realized that the saint, in all his greatness also had the powers of *Annapurna*.

# "People must have full faith in the Lord's *Leela.*"

Baba spent most of his time at the mosque and had devotees who visited him almost all day through. Once, a devotee while sitting near him noticed a lizard ticking on the wall. Wondering if this was a bad or good omen, he asked Baba, "Does the ticking of a lizard symbolise anything, Baba?"

Baba said, "The lizard is happy because her sister from the village of Aurangabad is coming to visit her today."

Upon hearing this, the man kept silent, not understanding Baba's words.

All of a sudden, a gentleman from Aurangabad came, and to the devotees' surprise, a lizard came out of his pouch. The lizard then rushed to meet the other lizard on the wall and it seemed as if the two were embracing each other. It was just as Baba had said.

This just goes to show the greatness of Sai Baba and the fact that he knows everything.

# "Abandon lust, wrath and avarice as they lead to self destruction."

Once a young man, who was selling pictures wanted to sell his pictures to a rich business man. The business man was always busy counting money and had no time for religion or God.

He asked him if he wanted to buy a picture of Sai Baba. The rich man, not being a devotee himself, was not very interested. However, he told the man that he would buy one for his son. His son was a firm devotee of Sai Baba and would like it if his father bought him one.

Busy counting money, he told him, "Take whatever money you need for the picture." The seller took one silver coin from the heap of coins and prepared to leave.

When the businessman saw this he stopped him and asked, "Why did you take just one coin? Surely the picture is worth more. Here, take more."

"I am not greedy," exclaimed the seller. "Sai Baba said that greed is man's enemy."

The businessman pondered on the reply and he finally felt ashamed of his thirst for money.

So he simply kept quiet and said, "Please rest for a while, have some water."

The young man however, politely refused and was just about to leave when the businessman's son entered. He saw the picture right away and was very happy to see that his father had bought the picture for him. Seeing the picture seller still there, he said "I have great faith in Baba and have always sought his guidance. Please have some refreshment."

"I cannot refuse such kindness from a fellow devotee," said the man.

After this meeting, the businessman realised his mistake and vowed to be a seeker of Truth and to cultivate loving devotion rather than yearn for wealth.

# "I speak the Truth, nothing but the Truth."

Sai Baba not only astonished the people with his miracles but by his presence and behaviour. There was once a time when a thief, on being caught for stealing attempted to blame Sai Baba of his crime. He had told the police that he did not steal the jewellery but it had been given to him by Sai Baba.

On hearing this, the police went to meet Sai to question him whether what the man was saying was true or not.

At the mosque, the police officer asked Sai,

"Do you vow to speak the truth?"

"I am the Truth," replied Sai, puzzling the police officer.

"Do you know the thief?" he continued.

"I know everyone," said Sai.

The policeman was perplexed by his answers and did not know what to say.

"What is your religion?"

"The religion of God."

Where did you come from?"

"I have come from the *Atma* (soul)."

"What is your caste?"

"The caste of the Divine."

The policeman was stupefied by Sai's answers. He realised that the replies were simple yet had a deep meaning. He understood that there was something divine about the man and that he was speaking the truth. He discontinued asking the questions and he left, bewildered by the saint's aura.

"Indeed, he is a saint," thought the policeman.

# "Believe Me, though I pass away."

In the Dwarkamai Masjid, there was an old brick which Baba always had with him. He used this brick to lean on while he was at *asana*.

One day, while Baba was not there, a man was sweeping the floor. When he saw the brick, he picked it up, thinking he would sweep the area where the brick lay as well. However, when he lifted the brick up, it slipped from his hands and fell to the ground. Just then Baba entered and saw the brick broken to pieces.

Baba could not bear to see the brick broken. Crying out loud, he said, "It is not just the brick that has shattered, but also my fate. This brick has been with me for years; it has been my friend; it was always with me whenever I have meditated. The end of this brick shows that my end too is drawing near!"

After that incident no one dared to question Baba about the brick. Soon after, however, they would see how important the brick was in Sai Baba's life!

83

Shirdi was in the grip of an epidemic and many people were dying. Baba's favourite disciple Tatya too, fell ill. He became very weak and his condition worsened each day. This saddened Sai Baba very much. People urged him to do something to cure Tatya soon, for it did not look as if he had much time to live. Baba knew that if he did not do anything, Tatya would die.

As he sat and looked at Tatya he remembered his promise to Bayaja and told the people, "Do not worry. From tomorrow onwards, Tatya shall start recovering." With that he walked away.

The next morning, Tatya indeed started recovering. Baba's powers were that great. However, when some devotees ran to the mosque to tell Baba that Tatya has improved, they found him in bed, still. He looked very weak and had high fever. Word that Sai Baba was not well spread like wildfire. All his devotees and followers became anxious. After three days, he was still sick. He stopped taking any food and had become thin and weak. While Baba's health worsened, Tatya's improved. The people understood that Sai was merely fulfilling the promise he made to Bayaja that he would protect Tatya even if it meant giving up his own life.

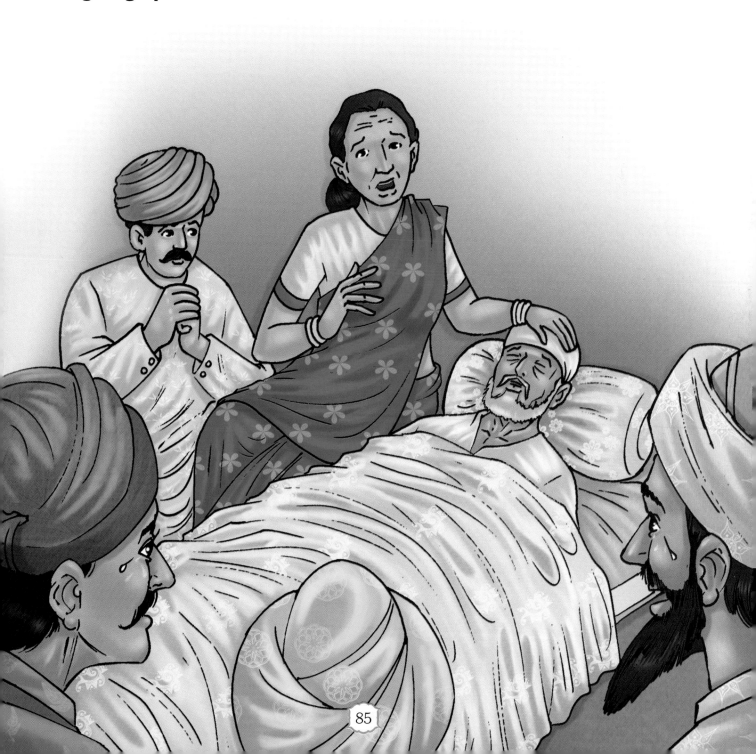

It had been days that Sai Baba had gone without food. None of his devotees dared to say anything.

One day, one of his most faithful devotees, Laxmi, could not take it anymore. She went, carrying a plate of food, and spoke to him, "Baba, it seems you no longer care about us. If you had you would not have fasted and would have ate and allowed yourself to get better. Please eat food, Baba. You cannot leave us." She cried as she spoke.

"The end is inevitable and my turn to depart is near. Please do not make my journey to the other end difficult. Instead, be happy for me for I shall be united with the Almighty," said Sai. "I don't have anything to give you but these few coins. Please take them and keep them. These nine coins represent the nine kinds of knowledge."

Laxmi took the coins and wept bitterly.

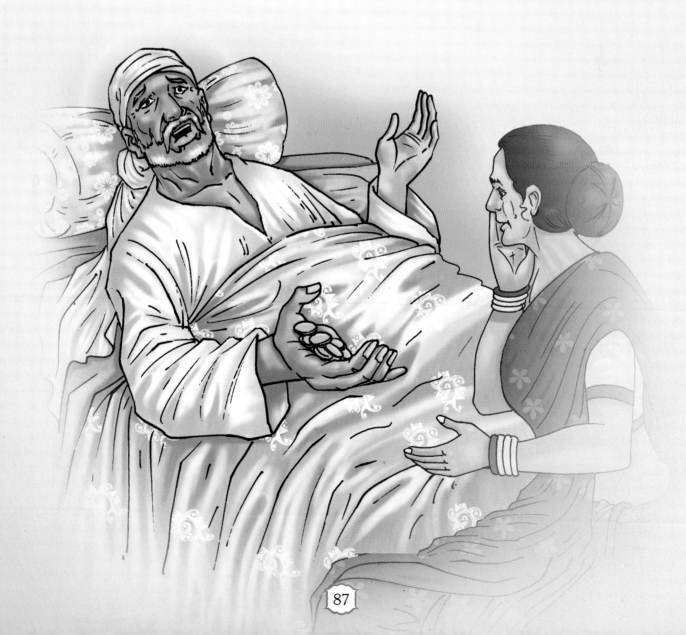

On the 15th of October, 1918, Baba left His body and entered *Maha Samadhi*. Crowds of people gathered to mourn his departure. Devotees from outside the village too went to Shirdi to pay their respects to Baba. However, they were consoled by the feeling that, for as long as they prayed and remembered his teachings, his name shall live on, and so shall his powers and miracles.

He was entombed in what we popularly now know as the *Samadhi Mandir*. Yet, he still continues to live within each and every one of his devotees.

Just as he had promised never to leave his devotees, he answers their prayers. His life, teachings and greatness is still remembered by the thousands who still visit his *Mandir*.

Chawri

Dwarkamai

Samad

ndir

Lendi Bagh

# Glossary

Annapurna – The Goddess who bestows Food

Asana – Yogic posture

Atma – Soul

Bhaktas – Devotees

Chawri – Village meeting hall. Baba used to spend a few hours over here and to sleep every alternate day at this place.

Darshan – The act of seeing a saint or a Guru.

Dhuni - a sacred fire maintained by Sai at the Dwarkamai mosque, from which he gave sacred ash to his devotees.

Fakir – A holy man.

Kafni - Long shirt extending to the knees

Kirtan - a devotional song in which lines are sung by a leader and then repeated by a large group.

Mahasamadhi – A word used when referring to the death or passing away of saints.

Mandir – Temple

Masjid – Mosque

Udi – The ash from the sacred fire at the Dwarkamai mosque.

Pooja – Worship and prayer.

Saburi – Patience

Shraddha – Faith

Tehsildar – Revenue collector

Zari – Golden lace